This book belongs to:

Tristan

Nemo

Dory

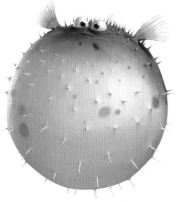

Bloat

STARRING

Gill

Marlin

This is a Parragon book
First published in 2006

Parragon
Queen Street House
4 Queen Street
Bath, BA1 1HE, UK

ISBN 978-1-4054-8014-7
Printed in China
Copyright © 2006 Disney Enterprises, Inc./Pixar Animation Studios

p

Marlin was a clownfish, but that didn't mean he had to find life funny. All he did was worry about his little son, Nemo. Marlin had lost his wife and more than four hundred eggs in a ruthless barracuda attack. Nemo had survived, but he had one damaged fin. Marlin was determined that no harm would ever come to his only son.

Nemo was a fun-loving fish who was looking forward to starting school and making new friends. But Marlin was so protective he didn't even like him going beyond their sea anemone home.

"What's the one thing we have to remember about the ocean?" he asked Nemo sternly.

"It's not safe," Nemo sighed.

On the first day of school, all the kids went on an outing to the edge of the reef. Nemo had made some new friends and they sneaked off together, daring each other to swim out into the open sea. Nemo was nervous and didn't venture very far, but it was way too far for Marlin, who was hovering nearby.

"You think you can
do these things but
you just can't, Nemo!"
Marlin yelled, rushing over.

Defiantly, Nemo decided to
prove him wrong. While his dad
was distracted, the little fish swam
out towards a boat anchored overhead.

Brave little Nemo had made it all the way to the boat when disaster struck – a scuba diver grabbed him!

"Daddy, help me!" yelled Nemo, as he was scooped up in a net.

"Coming, Nemo!" cried a distraught Marlin. There was nothing he wouldn't do to save his precious son. But Marlin couldn't catch up with the divers. Their boat sped off so fast that a diver's mask fell overboard.

A beautiful Regal Tang fish called Dory offered to help Marlin find Nemo, but unfortunately she had a short-term memory problem.

"I forget things almost instantly," she explained and promptly forgot who Marlin was. "Er...Can I help you?" she asked.

Marlin sighed and turned to go, only to come face to face with a shark!

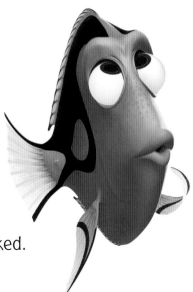

The shark was called Bruce. He was trying to be a vegetarian. The big bruiser wanted the fish to meet his like-minded buddies, so they could prove their motto: 'Fish are friends, not food!'

Dory, as enthusiastic as she was forgetful, thought the whole thing was a great idea. Marlin, who was totally terrified, did not!

The 'self-help' sharks held their meetings in a wrecked submarine. The meeting had already began.

"It has been three weeks since my last fish," Bruce told his friends proudly.

Always eager, Dory joined in. "I don't think I've ever eaten a fish," she said.

Just then, Marlin spotted the mask belonging to the diver who had taken Nemo! Dory wanted to show it to the sharks but Marlin didn't. As they tussled with the mask, Dory bumped her nose and it bled a little. Bruce got a sudden craving for a fish dinner!

A scary skirmish ensued before the plucky fish escaped with the mask in tow. But disaster struck when Dory accidentally dropped the mask into a deep ocean trench.

As they swam down after it, they were attracted to a pretty light dancing in the deep, dark water. It turned out to be the glowing antenna of a scary anglerfish just waiting to pounce!

While Marlin fought the fish, its light revealed an address written on the diver's mask. Luckily, Dory remembered that she could read!

"42 Wallaby Way, Sydney, Australia," she read.

Using the mask to trap the anglerfish, Marlin and Dory set off in search of the East Australian Current which would take them to Sydney – and Nemo!

Meanwhile, Nemo found himself in a dentist's fish tank in Sydney, where he met Bubbles, Peach, Jacques, Bloat, Deb, Gurgle and their leader, Gill.

Poor Nemo soon discovered how small the tank was. He could hardly swim any distance without hitting the sides. Worse still, Nemo learned that he was to be given to the dentist's niece, a ghastly girl named Darla. The tank fish were shocked.

"She's a fish-killer," whispered Peach.

Later that night, the fish asked Nemo to join their gang.

"If," Bloat whispered, "you are able to swim through THE RING OF FIRE!"

It sounded scary, but really it was just a trail of bubbles floating out of a fake volcano. Nemo bravely made it through and into the gang's hearts.

"We're all gonna get out of here," said Gill, and he began to tell the gang his plan.

Back in the ocean, Marlin and Dory
had swum into a forest of jellyfish.
They got badly stung trying to
bounce to safety on the tops of
the jellies and both passed out.
Sometime later, Marlin awoke
to find himself on the back of a turtle
named Crush. Marlin told Crush about
Nemo. "We need to find the East Australian Current," he said.
"You're riding it, dude!" laughed Crush, as they whizzed
along with the other turtles.

Tales of Marlin's adventures were spreading far and wide. Nigel, a friendly pelican who knew the Tank Gang, eventually heard the stories and rushed to tell Nemo the incredible news.

Nemo was amazed. He had always thought his dad was a bit of a scaredy-fish. The thought that he was battling his way to Sydney filled the little fish with pride.

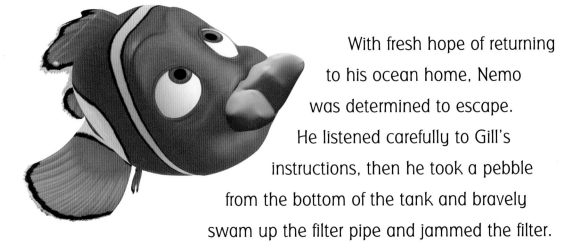

With fresh hope of returning
to his ocean home, Nemo
was determined to escape.
He listened carefully to Gill's
instructions, then he took a pebble
from the bottom of the tank and bravely
swam up the filter pipe and jammed the filter.

The water inside the tank gradually became green and filthy, but it was all part of Gill's plan. He reckoned the dentist would have to take the fish out of the tank to clean it. Then they simply had to wait to be put in bags on the counter. From there they could roll out of the window into the harbour below.

Back in the ocean, Marlin
and Dory said goodbye to the
turtles, but soon found themselves
swallowed up inside the mouth
of a massive whale.

"It's okay, I speak Whale," Dory assured
Marlin. "He either said we should move to the back
of his throat, or he wants a root beer float," she translated.

It turned out the whale was only giving the two brave little
fish a lift. They were soon squirted out of the whale's blow-hole,
right into Sydney harbour!

They nearly ended up as breakfast for a hungry pelican, but Nemo and Dory struggled so hard that he soon spat them out on to the dock. Luckily, Nigel rushed to their rescue.

"Hop inside my mouth if you want to live," he whispered to Marlin and Dory.

The weary fish realized they could either become lunch for a seagull, or trust the big pelican.

Scooping them up, Nigel flew over towards the dentist's surgery.

Inside, the dentist had cleaned the tank water with a fancy new automated cleaner – while the fish were still in the tank! The escape plan was ruined.

"What do we do when the little brat gets here?" worried Bloat.

But it was too late. Despite their efforts to save him, Nemo was lifted out of the tank and plopped into a bag. Darla had arrived. Nemo had one last chance – he played dead, hoping that he would get flushed down the toilet and out into the ocean.

Nigel stumbled through the window with Marlin and Dory just in time to see Nemo floating upside down in the plastic bag. The dentist quickly shooed Nigel away, but in the commotion he dropped Nemo. The bag burst open.

"I get a fishy!" squealed Darla as she reached out to grab him.

But the Tank Gang had
a plan. They launched
Gill out of the tank.

"Tell your dad I said hi!"
Gill yelled as he catapulted
the startled Nemo into the sink.

Once back in the tank, Gill
reassured his friends. "Don't worry.
All drains lead to the ocean."

Nigel flew back to the harbour and dropped a desolate Marlin and Dory in the water. Marlin thought he had lost Nemo for good and swam off to be on his own.

But then Dory found Nemo. She couldn't believe her eyes when she realized who the little orange clownfish was! Together, they swam after Marlin as fast as Nemo's little fins would let them.

There was a joyful reunion as Marlin realized how strong his son was and how overprotective he had been. He and Nemo had both learned that life was an adventure to be lived to the full.

Meanwhile, the Tank Gang were having an adventure of their own. They had finally made their escape. Now they just had to find a way to get out of the bags!